TWO GOOSE CREEK

RICHARD A. RAINWATER

Order this book online at www.trafford.com
or email orders@trafford.com

Most Trafford titles are also available at major online book retailers.

 www.trafford.com

North America & international
toll-free: 844 688 6899 (USA & Canada)
fax: 812 355 4082

Our mission is to efficiently provide the world's finest, most comprehensive book publishing service, enabling every author to experience success. To find out how to publish your book, your way, and have it available worldwide, visit us online at www.trafford.com

Because of the dynamic nature of the Internet, any web addresses or links contained in this book may have changed since publication and may no longer be valid. The views expressed in this work are solely those of the author and do not necessarily reflect the views of the publisher, and the publisher hereby disclaims any responsibility for them.

Adobe Stock images depicting people are used with their permission and for illustrative purposes only. Certain stock imagery © Adobe Stock.

ISBN: 978-1-6987-1644-2 (sc)
ISBN: 978-1-6987-1643-5 (e)

Library of Congress Control Number: 2024901886

Print information available on the last page.

Trafford rev. 01/25/2024

Two Goose Creek

God has lessons for each of us. They come in various forms. The spoken, the written through actions, and even nature itself. For three decades, I am the lone caretaker of our homestead. It was here that I was taught a great and marvelous lesson. One that I will never forget. As a young child, I learned this lesson. It was painful and with many regrets. I learned the lesson of true love.

CIRCA: 1915

An eight-year-old boy by the name of David Williams. He was doing his early morning chores when he heard hoof beats. David ran to the front of his house to see who was coming. Two soldiers on horseback rode up to David.

"We have a Western Union Telegram for a Mrs. Elaine Williams, can you tell us where she is?" the soldiers asked.

"She is in the house, I'll go get her." David went into the house and saw his mother washing dishes.

"Mommy there are two soldiers outside wanting to talk to you."

Elaine whispered under her breath, "Oh! My Lord." Slowly she walked to the door where the young man was standing. "I'm Mrs. Williams," she said tearfully.

One of the young soldiers walked toward her with an envelope in his hand. "This is from the War Department. It is in regards to your husband, Cpl. Jeffery Williams." He handed the letter to Mrs. Williams, turned, and got on their horses and left.

David's mother stood motionless as she looked at the letter. He knew something was wrong. Elaine's hand was shaking as she opened the envelope. The letter read,

February 12, 1915

RE: Corporal Jeffery Williams

Mrs. Williams,

Your husband has been wounded. The wounds are severe enough to warrant discharge. When well enough, will send state side then home.

Major Donald Van Meter

Days turned to weeks, weeks turned to months. We waited for news of Pa's return. Suddenly in October 1916, a wagon lumbered slowly down the road. We did not recognize the driver.

The wagon appeared to be empty. When the wagon drew near, David saw a head of a second person pop up in the back. David's mouth flew open. "It's Pa! It's Pa!"

Elaine was watching from the window. She burst from the front door with a smiling face and out reached arms; she ran to meet the wagon. Pa got up out of the wagon. He grabbed his wife and hugged and kissed her. He told her, "I missed you so much." Looking down he saw David looking up. "Well, there you are. You are almost grown."

Elaine grabbed hold of his face. "Look at me! You sorry thing for a husband, do you know how to write? We were both worried about you."

Mama said, "Come in and I will cook something. You are almost skin and bones. I will fatten you up in a hurry."

The next week or so was exciting. We had a barn dance and a party to celebrate Pa's safe return. Folks would travel for miles to shake the hand of a hero. I overheard a man ask Pa what war was like. I will never forget what Pa told him, "The war is over. I do not think or talk about it no more. You should not either."

****

The winter of 1916 through 1917 was a little bit on the hard side. Snow, howling winds, bitter cold, and the loss of stock. Pa received ten dollars a month for his wound in the war. Food and supplies were scarce.

One day like magic, the winter was gone and spring replaced it. The rebirth of the earth. The newly reunited family was busier than ever. Plowing and the planting of crops. Tending to the livestock and mending of the house and barn.

Over the space of time, praying and hoping, it was time for harvest. Planting has passed; now everything was full and ripe. It was a harvest of plenty. Pa would take his works to hand and sale or trade for things that were needed.

When the harvest was over, we could rest a few days. Pa went to town early in the morning. Momma said she had no idea where he was going or what he thought he was doing. Pa returned late that evening. David ran out to help him with the wagon.

Pa yelled and said, "Go back in the house and do not come back outside. Wait for me." After a while Pa came up the first steps, whistling.

He brought presents for both his wife and son. "Elaine, my darling, this is yours, a dress so pretty it will make all those old bittys at church green with envy." Elaine jumped up and screamed for joy, hugging him and kissing him.

"Now, David, this is yours." Pa reached in his duffel bag and pulled out a single shot .410 gauge shotgun and a box of shells.

David's eyes widened with amazement. "That's mine? Thank you so much for this." David smiled as he picked up his new gun. "Wow! How about that?"

Pa walked over and put his hand on David's shoulder. "Take care of your shells. Never shoot just to shoot. Always make your shot count."

Foreword 1979

Now I am old. I reflect back on the many lessons I have learned over the years. Several was hard to receive. But the lessons were learnt, even so harshly. So I decided to tell of one such lessons.

Both of my parents are now passed on. I did marry but only for a brief time. My wife died while in labor. The child was stillborn.

I still reside at the old homestead. Many memories still live here. I still have that old gun. It still stands in the corner of my closet. It was once very bright and shiny; now it is covered with a thick coat of dust. The shells are on the floor beside it. Paper that encased the shells have become faded and brittle. Minus only one, I fired only one shot.

When I am searching for something, I will brush up against it. Sometimes when moving things around, I see it. I will stare at it for a few moments and then maybe a tear in remembrance.

I still go down to the creek and visit the place where I learned a giant lesson. The creek itself had never had a name, at least I never heard of one. It holds a special meaning to me, and as long as I am alive, it will be forever be name TWO GOOSE CREEK!

Printed in the United States
by Baker & Taylor Publisher Services